Waitin
At Wuther

Waiting For Lulu
At Wuthering Heights

By
ANDY HOUSTOUN

Andy Houstoun is a philosophy teacher. He has had short stories published in a variety of magazines based in Great Britain, Australia and the USA, and has won three short story writing competitions. He lives in England with his wife and four children.

Illustration of 'Lulu'' on the front cover by Erin
Martin.

ISBN 9798511927923

Thanks to all those at the Scribophile writing community who critiqued early versions of many of the stories included in this book. Special thanks to Kathy Whipple, Antonia Rachel Ward, Curtis Bass, Paul Attmere, and Jennifer Ostromecki.

To the publications who had faith in my writing: Expat Press, Bright Flash Literary Review, Nauseated Drive, CaféLit, Ariel Chart Review, Spillwords, Adelaide, The Writing Quarter, Scrittura, Friday Flash Fiction, Madswirl, Scarlett Leaf Review, Pif magazine, Fiction On The Web, and the audio podcast Tall Tale TV.

To my family and friends for their encouragement: Josh, Dan, Zac, Si, Danola, Pete, Nic, 'Rudegirl' Rudie, Jase, Pete H, Zoe, Edie, Dustbunny, eris, Dave and Mazza. To those who inspired these stories: Emily Bronte,

Thomas Hardy, Johnny Cash, Robert Smith of
The Cure, Prince Rogers Nelson, the unknown
person who created the real Secret Garden, and
Carol 'Blondie' Martin.

Contents:

Introduction   17

Side 1

2021

Prologue   21

1979

The Man in Black   31

The Birthday Present   33

1986

Raspberry Beret   37

Free   41

Staring at the Stars   45

Heathcliff   49

The Killing Moon   53

Walk This Way   55

1991

The First Time   61

Nothing Else Matters   63

Midnight   67

How Do You Know?   69

1995

Waiting For Lulu   73

Lovesong   85

Side 2

Into the Lonely Night   97

His House   99

1997

The Secret Garden   103

Dear Auntie Ciara   109

The Bronte Guesthouse   113

Wuthering Heights   123

1999

Familiar Eyes   129

Hello   137

2021

Epilogue   143

Dedicated to Blondie

Introduction

During the Covid-19 lockdown of 2020 I wrote several short stories which were published in magazines and then in the book 'Short Stories of Love & Entanglement'.

Some of the stories featured the characters Dan and Lulu, and a few people suggested writing a flash novella on them. I wasn't sure what a flash novella was but discovered it's a collection of short stories that work by themselves but also link together to form a complete work.

It felt like it would work with my style of writing, and I was interested in going back to the childhoods of Dan and Lulu to explore what kind of things may have shaped their characters. It also enabled me to fill in a few gaps during their time together. So, here it is. A flash-novella about Dan and Lulu. 'Waiting For Lulu at Wuthering Heights.'

2021

Prologue

Two years ago, I created 'The Secret Garden'. I took some loose branches from the woodland in Sutton Park and set them up around the base of a cedar tree. Within them I left smile stones - large pebbles painted with patterns and images of things like hearts and eyes. I wrote uplifting words on them like: "Smile" and "Shine." In the middle I left a stone the size of a hand with these words painted on:

"This special garden is here for all to embrace.

Just be careful who you tell about this secret place."

Some people discovered it and moved the stones further up the path or into the forest for others to see. Over time, some added their own stones. One read: "RIP". Another: "Keep smiling."

In May, I took my daily walk through the park on a dull drizzly morning to see if any of the stones had been moved or new ones added. A piece of paper lay among the pebbles. It was enclosed in a plastic poly-pocket to keep it from getting wet and I could make out some writing on the front in blue ink: 'The Secret Garden'.

Intrigued, I picked it up and read:

"The Secret Garden inspired me to write a short story. It was published in the 'Black Ink Literary Review' and an alternative version is included in the book 'Waiting For Lulu at Wuthering Heights' by Dan McGregor.

I hope you like it.

D."

The story followed. I crouched down in the dampness of the leaves and read it there and then. In the tale, the writer captured the woodland walk and his discovery of the Secret Garden. He went on to describe a note left there. The note reminded him of a past relationship at university. A girl called Lulu. The story of their romance followed and intrigued me.

After finishing the story, I replaced it in the poly-pocket and continued home, pleased that my creation had inspired a piece of writing.

When I got in, I searched for the story on the Black Ink Literary Review website and found 'The Secret Garden' immortalised in print.

I searched for the author's book and bought a copy. The next day, I brewed a cup of tea and sat back to read.

Side 1

"If all else perished, and he remained, I should still continue to be; and if all else remained, and he were annihilated, the universe would turn to a mighty stranger." - Wuthering Heights by Emily Brontë

1979

The Man in Black

Dan knows how to play a record without scratching it, even though he's only nine years old.

The vinyl disc slides out of the paper sleeve, and he holds it with his thumb on the edge and his fingers on the label just the way his dad taught him.

"You need to protect the surface from dust and marks."

He places it on the turntable, finding the centre so it slips into position on the soft plastic platter.

He presses the silver 'play' button and the disc spins just like it has done so many times before. The arm moves across. It touches the record with a crackle, and the familiar cheering from Folsom Prison rises through the speakers. Johnny Cash introduces himself and the twanging guitar intro to 'Folsom Prison Blues' bounces into the room.

Dan sits back against the edge of his bed and a tear slides down his face. It's a year since his dad died.

THE END.

The Birthday Present

Walking into the kitchen, Lulu runs the miniature plastic brush through her doll's hair. Her eighth birthday present.

She looks up and freezes. "Ma?" The doll falls.

Her mum lays in a heap by the sink with bare legs sprawled over cold quarry tiles.

Lulu runs forward and pulls the dressing gown over naked thighs. "Ma?"

She removes the glass bottle from the woman's hand and there's an incoherent mumble in response. She pushes the tangled mess of hair away from her mother's face where the vomit is.

It's congealed with saliva and smells of puke and alcohol.

Taking a cloth from the sink, she runs it over her mother's cheeks. "Ma? Are y'all right?"

With heavy breathing she runs to the hallway, picks up the phone and dials 999.

THE END.

1986

Raspberry Beret

The record cover shows a painted image of a woman dressed in a black dress and a raspberry beret, holding an apple in one hand. The background is made up of random shapes in green, pink, purple and black. Prince's latest single.

Dan has bought everything Prince has released, ever since seeing the music video for '1999'. He's spent all his money on anything Prince-related. Every album, single, and music magazine that has featured him.

He removes the plastic disc from the sleeve. It slides out into his hand, and he inspects the label. Multi-coloured cursive words say: 'Prince & The Revolution.' The other side is light blue with painted clouds and the words: 'Raspberry Beret.'

He places the record on the turntable, it spins, and the needle touches the vinyl. The rhythm of a drum-machine pounds through the speakers into his bedroom, the voice of Prince counts to four, and Dan is lost in the twirling sounds of violins playing in harmony with cellos.

Prince's voice tells the story of working in a five-and-dime. Dan isn't sure what the American term means but thinks it might be like his experience working in the butcher's shop every Saturday.

Prince sings about not getting on with his boss. Dan knows what it's like to work in a job that doesn't inspire him.

Then the singers magical voice tells of a girl who walks in through the 'OUT' door wearing a raspberry beret. He falls in love with her. She's dressed in the type of clothes you might find in a second-hand shop.

Dan is sure that one day he will meet a girl like that. An unconventional girl who will turn his life upside down. He wants it more than anything.

THE END.

Free

Lulu removes a plastic Safeway bag from the bin. It's covered in a yellow liquid and loose coffee granules. Her nose wrinkles in disgust as the smell of rotten garbage and vegetables rises towards her. There. Underneath some apple peelings, the edge of the cassette case juts out. She takes it.

It's in remarkably good condition. Like new. She opens it to check the mechanism. It reminds her of yesterday when she bought it in HMV and held it for the first time with the excitement of getting back to the orphanage to listen.

She pulls at some more rubbish. The scrunched-up card lays at the edge. She takes it and hand-presses the creases to see the words: 'Purple Rain' and Prince staring back from his motorbike surrounded by smoke and a dark city street.

She reaches further into the bin and feels the plastic cassette. A smile crosses her face, and she takes it out of the dirty pit. Fragile tape hangs from the bottom in a tangled mess but turning one of the cogs moves it back into the cassette. She turns it some more and it twists the wrong way but by stopping and easing it back into position she can guide it back in. It's not perfect but it might still play.

Since living here, Lulu has struggled. There are no children she can relate to, and the nuns constantly reprimand her. She finds solace in music. She hides a Walkman under her pillow and listens to it at night through headphones. It takes her to another world.

She recalls Sister Madeline's outraged expression when she found the tape in Lulu's bag that afternoon.

"This filth is banned!" It had been confiscated immediately.

 Lulu can't understand why she isn't allowed to listen to Prince. She's allowed to read The Bible. She reads about Jesus and how he stands up for outsiders and speaks of freedom for the oppressed, but the nuns have a more authoritarian understanding God.

 Prince sings about being free. One day Lulu will be free from this place and find someone to love her.

THE END

Staring at the stars

The end of the cigarette glows orange as Dan takes a long drag. He exhales into the night sky. "Apparently there's billions of them. You just can't see them in the city because of the streetlights."

"Is that right?" Greg sits next to him. They're on a tin roof below Dan's bedroom window, with their backs against the brick wall.

"They're lightyears away."

"What even is a lightyear?"

"Weren't you paying attention in Mr. Johnston's

physics lesson?"

"I was too busy looking at Isabella Woodward's legs."

Dan shakes his head. "It's the distance light travels in a year. Something like 100 000 miles a second." He points his fingers and moves his hand across the sky, "So, if you travel at that speed for a year, that's a lightyear. Mind-blowing, isn't it?"

"Not as mind-blowing as Isabella Woodward's legs. Apparently, she's been asking about you. Are you going to ask her out?"

Dan sighs. "No."

"What's wrong with you? Are you gay or something?"

"She's not my type."

"Not your type?"

"There's no spark."

"What do you mean no spark? Have you seen her legs?"

"There's no…chemistry there."

"Well, chemistry or no chemistry, I'd be in there at lightspeed if I was you."

Dan stubs his cigarette out on the metal roof and the orange glow disappears. "Where do you think we'll be in ten years' time?"

"Well, I'll be married to Isabella Woodward, and you'll be sitting somewhere by yourself, staring at the stars."

THE END.

Heathcliff

Steam rises from the cup of tea into the autumn air. Lulu sits in the orphanage garden warming her hands on the cup.

Two swallows glide across the clear sky. There's the hum of a vehicle in the distance and then it dies away leaving the echo of birdsong in the surrounding trees.

"There's a present for you here!"

Lulu creases her brow and looks back at Sister Ashleigh stepping through the back door.

"For me?"

"It's from your Auntie Ciara."

Lulu takes the gift in her hand. It's wrapped in newspaper and rips off easily.

'What is it?" Sister Ashleigh looks over her glasses.

"The Mayor of Casterbridge," Lulu glances at the titles of the books in her hand, "and Wuthering Heights."

"Wonderful."

"Wuthering Heights?"

"I think you'll like that one."

"What's it about?"

"An orphan called Heathcliff."

"What happens to him?"

"He gets adopted by an English family. He has a hard time with his adopted brother but forms a special bond with the sister Kathy."

"Go on."

"The dad dies, and the brother treats Heathcliff very badly, but him and Kathy become close. They share an almost supernatural connection. What is it she says? 'Whatever our souls are made of, his and mine are the same'. It's full of lots of poetic images."

"So do they end up living happy ever after?"

"No. Kathy meets someone else and ends up marrying him."

"What?"

"You'll have to read it Lulu. You'll get a lot out of it. It's beautifully written."

Lulu opens the cover and smells the fresh pages. She looks forward to losing herself in the story.

THE END.

The Killing Moon

Orange streetlamps and misty fog give the road a dreamlike ambience. Dan pushes off into the centre of the street and cycles past parked cars and leafy trees.

'The Killing Moon' by Echo & The Bunnymen plays through his headphones as he makes his way up Highbridge Road Hill.

Gliding down the other side, he swerves left and right. The air is sweet with cherry blossom and the rush of air blows his hair around his face. White road markings flash under his tyres and he peddles hard in fifth gear. He's in a movie with a magical soundtrack, while the rest of the world sleeps.

THE END.

Walk This Way

Lulu pushes up the window. There's a creak from outside the bedroom door behind her and she freezes.

Silence.

She squeezes through the space between the windowsill and the bottom of the frame onto the roof of the bay window. The surface is rough under her bare feet. The air is still, the sky dark.

Lulu holds onto the branch of a tree that hangs near the window and climbs along another one towards the trunk. She eases herself down to the ground and onto the grass. It's damp and cold under her feet as she wanders over to the back of the garden behind some bushes, out of sight of the orphanage.

She presses the play button on her Walkman and a strong rhythm pounds through her headphones. Lulu holds the headset over her ears and nods her head in time to the music. Run DMC rap along to the beat, and Lulu moves her body to the sound.

She steps backwards and forwards in time to the music across the grass in her nightshirt. Her body becomes more energetic as she falls into the groove of the song. She's in a music video.

Out of the bushes, dancers emerge dressed in gold sequined bikinis and high heels, heavy make-up, and peacock feathers in their hair. They dance around her. Young men in tracksuits and gold chains around their necks appear on the other side of the garden and jump around to the song. A man in a top hat carrying a big bass drum stomps passed, pounding along to the rhythm, and more dancers appear.

Jam Master Jay scratches a record on a turntable by the hedge, producing more percussive sounds. Run and DMC appear next to her and leap around to the sound of the drum machines and heavy guitars, singing with

everything they've got. Lulu dances behind
them, consumed in the music.

THE END.

1991

The First Time

Dan's in The Jug of Ale with Coddy. It's crowded; music thumping, lights flashing, everywhere the cacophonous din of laughter and chatting.

"Hey, Dan." Coddy nudges him, pointing to a girl on the dancefloor. "What do you think of her?"

Dan isn't sure who he means. Most of the girls are dressed the same - short skirts and white stilettos.

"Yeah...she looks all right." It's not Dan's kind of

venue.

He spends most of the night slowly nursing a pint of Guinness while Coddy does his best to impress any female who will listen to him. He manages to speak to a girl with long dark hair.

"So, what do you do?" she asks.

"I'm an astronaut," Coddy says with straight-faced confidence.

Then Dan sees a girl walk up to the bar. She wears a purple, knee-length dress with Doc Marten boots, but what draws her to him are her eyes. They're dark, glistening with life.

THE END.

Nothing Else Matters

He lives in the attic of a Victorian house in a cheap part of Birmingham. It's full of canvases and books with titles like 'Searching For God Knows What' and 'What's So Amazing About Grace?'

A record-player sits on a guitar amplifier in the corner. Records lean against the wall. Echo & The Bunnymen, U2, The Cure.

They eat together and share a bottle of wine.

"Where abouts in Ireland are you from?" Dan asks her.

"Limerick."

"Sounds nice."

"Not really. I was brought up in a Catholic orphanage."

Dan looks at her with interest and she continues: "My dad left us when I was eight. My mum didn't cope very well, and they took me off her a few months later. I didn't want to go, but they dragged me, kicking and screaming." She laughs at the thought of her eight-year-old self so passionate and determined.

"Have you seen your mum or dad since then?"

"I don't think they'd be interested. All I know is I don't want to be left by anyone again. I prefer not to get too close to people."

She downs the rest of her drink in one. "I'm no good, Dan. I'm no good for anyone. My mum told me; the nuns told me. It's all I ever heard." Her voice breaks and her head hangs.

She feels his hand on her shoulder. He moves the glass away from her and touches her face.

Their lips touch, and for a moment, nothing else matters.

THE END.

Midnight

Dan and Lulu sit under cloudless blue skies outside their tent in the long grass. They survey the endless Haworth moors - the setting of Lulu's favorite book 'Wuthering Heights'.

"It's beautiful," she says.

"It is." Dan breathes in the warm summer air.

'Lovesong' by The Cure comes on the stereo Lulu has brought along. Dan pulls her to her feet, and they dance close, surrounded by endless hills.

"When you hear this song, think of me," he says.

He wants to ask her to marry him but fears being turned down. Instead, he says: "Do you think we'll still be together in five years?"

"Maybe." She smiles, amused at his question.

And then, to try and ensure they don't ever lose contact, he comes up with an idea: "Let's meet back here on my twenty-fifth birthday, whether we are or not. Midnight."

"Okay." She smiles and looks deep into his eyes.

He holds the side of her face in his hand and reaches towards her. Two souls merge; the outside world becomes non-existent. Bodies touch; stir.

THE END.

How Do You Know?

"How do you know if you've found the person you want to marry?" Lulu asks Dan.

They're both working on paintings in his room. His, a self-portrait with a dark, industrial background. Hers, an image of herself without hair, curled in the foetal position.

Portishead plays on the record-player.

He looks up. "If it feels right, I guess."

"But what if you're not sure? How do you know?"

"Maybe it takes a while?"

THE END.

1995

Waiting For Lulu

Dan sits in The Wuthering Heights pub. It's a
shameless exploitation of the novel's title but
Lulu and he didn't care when they stumbled
across the place a few years ago. They liked the
way it blatantly took advantage of its location on
the edge of the remote Haworth moorland. They
had dinner here before setting off into the open
country with their tent and camping equipment.

Tonight, Dan finishes his meal alone. He
undoes the top button of his shirt and releases

the pressure around his neck. He removes his Anglican clerical collar and places it on the table. He's the only customer. Heavy snow has left the place empty.

He looks towards the door, half expecting Lulu to walk in, but he knows it's unlikely. It's been over three years since he's seen her.

He reaches into his shirt pocket for a picture of her, taken in her student house. Her eyes stare back, wild and dark. Her pale skin is unblemished, with naturally pink cheeks. Blonde hair cropped short at the back and long at the front, hangs down to her jawline on one side. She changed the colour frequently, but blonde suited her best. She's wearing a T-shirt from the Cure's Brixton Academy gig. Robert Smith's face is stretched across her chest, and at the bottom in red are the words: 'MIXED UP'. Behind her, scrawled over the walls in black ink, are verses of her poetry. She never stopped writing: in notebooks, on scraps of paper, on her hands, wherever she was, whenever she thought of it. She even wrote one on the back of this photo. He studies the familiar words:

It's a picture of a house I built burning in my head,

It's a picture of a little boy bouncing on a bed,

It's a picture of a little girl bouncing by his side,

It's a picture of a daddy who may as well have died.

He turns it back over. There's a white fold-line across the middle of the photo, but it's the only picture he has of her. He places it on the table next to his dog-collar.

Outside, snowflakes

tumble

down

in ever-changing

courses.

Fleeting shapes

fall

and disintegrate on the glass before his eyes
can catch them. More

drift

down

against the winter landscape.

***

"Your bill, sir!"

The waiter places his bill on the table. Two men stand by the door, ready to lock up for the night. A glance at his watch tells Dan it's midnight. He apologizes for keeping them, puts his collar and photo in his pocket, and settles up. He steps outside.

It's stopped snowing and the wind has died down. Everything is white.

He pulls his coat collar tight around his neck and wanders along the path towards the heath, the inspiration for Emily Brontë's tragic love story.

A single snowflake lands on his nose. Then another. He looks up at the night sky as the snow starts to fall again. He pulls back his coat sleeve and checks his watch. It's ten past midnight. He wanders further down the lane.

"Like the eternal rocks beneath."

That's how Lulu once described her love for him, and he felt the same. He'd never met anyone so fearless and unpredictable, yet introspective and thoughtful. They had been together for more than a year, spending every available moment with each other.

He walks through the falling snow, along a dim, deserted path in the direction of the rock face, close to where they camped. From the gate on his right, the lane slopes towards the open countryside. He sinks up to his calves in soft, fresh snow. All he can hear is his own breathing and the light crunch of each step as he moves forward.

She gave no explanation when she left except, she needed to get her head straight. A week afterwards, he received a poem from her in the post, along with a note saying she was staying with an aunt in Ireland. A few weeks after that, the lease ran out on his house. He tried everything to get in touch with her, but no-one could help. The university wouldn't provide him with any information, and no-one knew her home address or even which village she was from. He never heard from her again.

He arrives at a steep bank and the snow slides away in clumps. He grabs a branch above his head and a dusting of white powder falls, but he's made it. He's in an open space with a view of endless hills. He stands for a long time, taking it all in, looking for any sign of life on the beautiful, desolate moor.

He spent a few months drinking himself into a numb haze when she left, until he realised he was better off getting his life back on track, training for the ministry, helping all those other brokenhearted people.

Dan's been the rector at St Matthews in Haworth for a year. None of the leadership or parishioners know anything about Lulu. He takes a deep breath. Tonight, he hopes to put old ghosts to rest. The air is crisp and still. Nearby, branches crack as they strain under the weight of fresh snow. He stands motionless on the moor, listening.

A memory comes to mind. A tree they discovered. It had been struck by lightning. All that was left was the remains of the trunk, the top brown and charred.

Lulu had taken out a penknife. It was about five centimeters long with a shamrock on the side. "This is the only thing I have that belonged to my mom," she told him. "It's not good for much but I use it for my art sometimes."

She had crouched in the grass and carved into the trunk:

'Lovesong

Think of me

Always'

He's not far from the place.

He steps forward.

Around the side of a hill is the towering rock face they climbed. At the top they held each other, surrounded by endless countryside. He stands motionless, absorbed by the familiar sight, and it feels like she's there with him.

Another memory unfolds. Something she said to him. A Brontë quote. What was it? He closes his eyes to concentrate. There was a moment when Lulu slipped from his arms and looked straight at him:

"Be with me always - take any form - drive me mad! Only do not leave me in this abyss, where I cannot find you!"

He opens his eyes. The seriousness of her face when she said it. And yet here he is, back on the heath, unable to find her.

Praying feels pointless. He reaches into his coat pocket and takes out a small bottle of Glenlivet. There's a crack as he twists off the cap. He holds the bottle to his mouth and takes a generous gulp. The acrid taste of scotch burns the back of his throat. His eyes are warm with tears and he throws the bottle as hard as he can onto the heath. It lands with a quiet thud and disappears into the snow.

Dan stumbles backwards a moment and through blurred vision, sees the burned-out tree. Such a distinctive sight. One side is covered in snow and the other untouched. He walks towards it and sees the familiar words:

'Lovesong

Think of me

Always'

They've faded but are still visible. He runs his
fingers over the indentations and reaches into
his pocket. He takes out Lulu's penknife.

A warm tear

          rolls

             down

                  his cold face.

THE END.

Lovesong

A pound coin

      clatters

            down

                the slot.

An image of Lulu's face and blond hair reflects on the glass front of the old jukebox. She scrolls through the song choices and punches in 7-3-5.

A seven inch of The Cure's 'Lovesong' moves into position. The tonearm slides across and there's a crackle as the needle settles into the grooves.

A distorted guitar chord erupts from the speakers into the empty pub, and the familiar driving rhythm starts. The church-like organ, the bouncing bass, and the jangly guitar, churn up feelings that stir Lulu's heart.

She's in The Wuthering Heights pub. She goes back to her seat and glances around the room.

It still has the same decor: lead-framed windows and ornate mirrors; paintings of the Yorkshire landscape in gilt frames. The smell of real ale and stagnant smoke.

She's twenty again.

She stares at the door and imagines Dan walking in. She hasn't seen him for years.

As 'Lovesong' plays on, she takes out a letter. She found it in the pocket of her coat when she put it on this morning. She planned to send it years ago. She looks at her familiar handwriting:

"Dear Dan,

I'm so sorry.

I shouldn't have left you the way I did.

My feelings were becoming too intense, and I couldn't handle them.

I know I should have explained things better, but I was struggling so much. At the time it was easier to just..."

Tear stains distort the next letters and that's where it ends. She didn't even know she still had the letter until this morning.

Things were so different the last time they were here. She remembers Dan's words: "Let's meet back here on my twenty-fifth birthday, no matter what. At midnight."

She was hesitant. It was a crazy idea, but she said: "Okay."

A glance at the clock behind the bar tells her it's ten past twelve. There's no sign of Dan. It dawns on her that midnight could mean the turn of midnight first thing in the morning, or it could mean now - the night of his birthday.

Is it possible that he's already been? He might have gone straight to the place where they camped.

She gathers her coat and steps outside into the cold night air. There's not a sound except for the faint whisper of snowflakes landing all around her. The moon is big and bright.

She pulls her hat down over her ears and trudges down the lane in the direction of where they pitched their tent. In the silence, as she sets off, the crunch of her footsteps is deafening.

Snowflakes begin to fall like confetti as she walks along the deserted path, and more memories unfold.

Dancing together on the moor. The smell of aftershave on his neck. The laughter in his eyes.

She hears the muffled sound of voices and a television from inside a farmhouse as she passes by. A lantern hanging from the stone wall glistens in the cold night air. The noise from the house dies away as she walks on.

When she left Dan, she told him she needed to get her head straight. She went back to Ireland and stayed with her aunt and spent months working on paintings and poetry. Hardly left her room. She wrote to him. She kept writing for months but never heard back. She doesn't blame him. He was probably fed up with her. Maybe he found himself a nice sensible girl.

She stops for a moment and stands motionless, looking at the distant hills covered in thick snow. The moon is hidden behind a streak of cloud and her mind wanders back to yesterday morning:

"Where is it, you're off to?" her aunt asked.

"Yorkshire."

"What are you going there for?"

"To visit an old friend."

Her aunt paused and said: "Have you ever thought at all about settling down, Lulu?"

Lulu smiled and sighed. "There was someone once but it didn't work out."

"Have you considered dating anyone else? Rob's been asking after you a lot. He's a handsome man and he'd make a lovely husband."

Rob was a family friend. He was sweet, but she couldn't lead him on with Dan on her mind.

She shook her head. "I'm not ready."

***

Moonlight shines through the clouds and her eyes become accustomed to the light reflecting off the heath. Apart from black shadows under bushes, everything seems as bright as daylight. She hears a faint crackle and feels a chill on her neck, listening intently. She can sense someone near. Close behind her. Maybe two meters away. Maybe closer. She's too scared to turn. A rustle. Someone out walking their dog, perhaps? Or is it the sound of winter on the moors?

"Dan?"

She turns, but there's not a soul for miles. It's stopped snowing.

She takes out an MP3 player and finds their song. She puts the headphones in her ears and presses play. That desperate guitar-chord. She closes her eyes and loses herself in the pulsating rhythm and Robert Smith's melancholy voice.

When she opens her eyes, all she can see is a desolate landscape.

"Don't leave me in this abyss," she whispers.

She turns and sees a tree she recognises. It had been struck by lightning giving it an unusual shape. "That is so rare," she remembers Dan saying.

There's nothing left of one side except for the trunk. She had taken a penknife and carved words into it. Such a distinct memory.

She wanders closer and sees the words:

'Lovesong

Think of me

Always'

And underneath, are more:

'If only

you'd come

Dan

X'

THE END.

Side 2

Into The Lonely Night

Dan sees her.

She's standing on the other side of the German market by the wooden nativity scene. The neon star's aura shines over the long cream coat he bought her last Christmas.

"Lulu!" Dan's voice is drowned out by bustling customers and Nat King Cole crooning 'Unforgettable' through nearby speakers.

Frantically, he squeezes through the crowd, enveloped by the smell of damp clothes, mulled wine, and cinnamon.

As he reaches the path, breathless, he catches a glimpse of her hand closing a taxi door, and watches the rear lights disappear into the lonely night.

THE END.

His House

Lulu walks past his house

hoping he might see her

and come out

even though he moved

years ago.

"I wonder where he is now?"

THE END.

1997

The Secret Garden

Sunlight reflects on the surface of the lake in the distance as Dan walks through the dark trees of the forest. Sticks snap under his heavy boots and he breathes in the scent of decomposing leaves and pine needles. When he arrives at the water's edge, he stops. A range of purple trees are visible on the far side. Beautiful.

He whistles and listens for a response. A few seconds later a creature darts through the trees behind him.

"Billie!"

His dog, a cross between a Hungarian Vizsla and a Collie, leaps into the air next to him, then races back into the woods over some bushes.

Dan walks on along the path circumnavigating the lake. There's no wind this morning and it's not as cold as it has been in recent days.

He passes a fallen elm. Its long trunk and branches protrude into the water, reflecting on the still surface in perfect symmetry. He steps around a mire and heads towards the woodland. Billie runs ahead.

A tree with the shape of an eye patterned in the bark, looks down at him as he steps onto the bank at the edge of the forest and heads into the trees. He likes to get off the main path. There's less marsh ground and the chances of running into anyone is unlikely.

Here, thousands of fallen leaves have turned the ground into a soft carpet of orange. Through some thorn bushes he finds himself in an open area where tree trunks stretch upwards like columns of a cathedral. A little further on and he's at the Secret Garden. Dozens of sticks form a fence around the base of a tree and within them is a collection of stones painted in bright colours. One has the image of smiling lips. Another a heart. One says: "RIP". In the middle is a brown pebble the size of a hand with neat, white painted writing: "The Secret Garden."

He came across it the day of his interview at St. Matthews Church. It lifted his spirits. One stone in particular: "Shine," painted in yellow next to an image of the sun. It encouraged him to do just that. The vicar's job was offered to him later that day. He's been living here three years now and always starts the day walking around the lake. It clears his head, and wears Billie out.

The day after his interview, he took the stone and placed it on another part of his route by the side of the path. He wanted to pass the message on, and for the person who painted it to know it had been seen.

Another day he saw a stone with the words: "Be Kind". Further along his route he came to a marshland and dragged a fallen branch over to make a bridge. He wanted to add to the positive spirit of this rare place that hardly anyone else knew about.

He found more. As he made his way through a particularly unapproachable part of the woods, many fallen trees lined the ground and had to be climbed over. The bushes were closer together and more difficult to pass. He saw something red and white beyond, resting on the branch of a tree but couldn't work out what it was at first. It looked like it might be a cap or a piece of clothing. He climbed closer to see an envelope.

The damp paper was delicate in his hands. He opened it and read: "This special garden is here for all to embrace. Just be careful who you tell about this secret place."

The words reminded him of Lulu. She wrote poetry all the time. Some of it like this. Enigmatic, with an ability to touch you. His gut stirred. It couldn't be her surely. She left to live in Ireland. He placed the letter back in the envelope.

"Billie! Come on!"

He didn't see anything new for many months but three days ago discovered a glove on the ground under a shrub. An adult's glove. Pink. He picked it up and placed it on a branch in the centre of the open area.

The next day it was replaced by a note saying: "Thank you."

Dan wonders if there's anything today.

A stone on the ground with a painted red arrow points up the hill. He presses on up the steep bank where the trees are closer together. He pushes his way through a holly bush, protecting his skin by pushing his shoulder into the branches. There in front of him are more stones. They form a pathway on the ground, with candles painted on them. At the end is another envelope sitting on the bough of an oak tree. Dan opens it and reads the words:

"I don't know who you are, but I wish you well. You're clearly a kind person and it's good to know there are kind people out there. I'm leaving tomorrow, but before I go, I want you to know

that I appreciated your kindness. I pray that you
will find happiness wherever you end up.

L

X."

THE END

Dear Auntie Ciara

Lulu drops her rucksack on a seat and takes the position next to the window of the bus. In the darkness, and the rigmarole of deciding on the best place to sit, she's unsure how many other people are onboard. She smells coffee.

Looking up she sees a switch above her head and clicks it on to give herself some light.

There's a hiss from the door as it closes, and the bus moves forward out of the station.

Lulu reaches into her rucksack and rummages for a notebook and pen. She pauses a moment, holding the pen against her lips and then she writes:

"Dear Auntie Ciara,

Thank you for persuading me to return to Haworth. It's been beautiful. I'm now heading home.

The hotel you booked for me was right next to a lake. I could walk there whenever I felt like it. My room was called the 'Emily Bronte' and it had paintings of scenes from Wuthering Heights on the walls. I loved it.

I visited the Bronte Museum again and the house where the Brontes lived.

The scenery around here is stunning and gave me a chance to think things through and clear my head a little.

I've written lots of new poetry.

I've also decided to say yes to Rob. While I can't stop thinking about Dan, I realise that the chances of ever seeing him again are tiny and I can't waste my life hoping for something that will never happen."

Lulu's eyes well up and her throat tightens. She switches the overhead light off, turns her face to the window and lets the tears come.

THE END.

The Bronte Guesthouse

There are no hotels anywhere near the Secret Garden except for one. A three-story guesthouse stands alone at the end of a sandy dirt-track.

Dan enters the front door and is greeted by a woman who looks to be in her forties. Her auburn hair is gathered at the back and secured at the top of her head with a butterfly clip.

Dan approaches. "Morning, I don't know if you can help me. I'm looking for someone called Lulu. I thought she might be staying here."

The receptionist looks at his clerical collar and smiles. "Lulu. A blonde girl?"

"Yeah, that's her. Lulu O'Connell."

"She left yesterday."

"Yesterday?"

"Yes, back to Ireland I believe."

Dan catches his breathe. "I don't suppose you've got an address for her, have you?"

"Ah now, even if I did, we're not allowed to give out that kind of information I'm afraid. I'm sorry I'm no help."

Dan pauses a moment. "How long was she

here? If you don't mind me asking."

"Two weeks."

Is there any way he can find her?

The receptionist speaks: "The room she stayed in is free now for the next few days if you're interested."

"Yes, please. I'll book one night. I just need to gather a few things and I'll return this evening. Thank you."

***

It's late at night by the time Dan gets back to the guesthouse. The receptionist pushes open a wooden door which leads into a huge space with high-reaching ceilings and white painted walls. Wooden floorboards stretch the expanse of the area leading to tall patio doors where the back garden is faintly visible through muslin curtains. Picture frames hang on the walls with paintings of scenes from Wuthering Heights.

Amongst various pieces of oak furniture, a king-sized brass bed takes up one corner and in another stands a shelving unit holding dozens of books.

"I'm sure you'll love it here. Lulu did."

"Thanks."

"Lovely girl, if a little dreamy." She smiles. "But that's poets for you."

"Dreamy?"

"Artists are funny folk. I saw her wandering round the garden one night. Must have been about three in the morning, lost in thought. Anyway, I'll leave you be. Enjoy your stay."

"Thank you."

Lulu was here yesterday. In this room.

Dan glances at the pictures on the wall, removes his shoes and jacket and carries them to the wardrobe. As he opens the tall thin door, he hears something tumble to the floor. A small notebook. He picks it up and inspects the black cover, patterned in pink roses. It contains scribblings and doodles. Poetry. Lulu's poetry. Sitting on the bed, he reads:

'With a ready heart, I swore
To give my spirit to adore
You, ever present, phantom thing,
My slave, my poet, and my king."

The verses speak of solitude and loneliness and a need for deep connection.

'My heart longs for a touch divine,
And for another soul to find
Me here, beside the wild sea,

To cherish and to comfort me.'

He turns to the back to see if there's an address, a place name, anything, but it just contains poetry.

He places the notebook on the bed and walks to the backdoor. A silvery light shines through the ghost-like curtains. He pulls back the drapes and looks at the garden. The bright moon gives the world a strange grey hue. He turns the key slowly so as not to wake anyone and steps outside. The clear air is perfectly still. He steps onto the lawn and makes his way towards the shadowed woodland at the end of the garden. Dewy grass clings to his bare feet.

Such a beautiful night, and Lulu was walking around here a few days ago.

A small creature startles him and scuttles over the grass into the undergrowth. Leaves stir on the bushes, and he turns to look back at the house. There's one light on upstairs. Dan stands a while and is about to go back when he notices a dark figure move through the trees and disappear into the blackness.

Lulu? She can't be here, surely. She's gone back to Ireland.

There again, further on, a woman wearing a thin white gown walks towards the lake. Dan hears the gentle ripple of the water, and the woman sits on a sandy bank. Her hands support her body as she leans back.

Who is she? What is she doing out at this time of night?

He stands a while, watching. Water glides in on a strong current and washes under her, but she stays where she is. Taking a deep breathe, she tilts her head back into the night sky.

"Lulu?"

A cloud covers the moon, and Dan glances around. When he looks back, she's gone.

He rushes through the woodland to the place where she was but there's no sign of anyone.

The forest trees have lost their colour in the dimness of the night and there's not a sound except for the calm lake. He fills his lungs with the warm spring air, the faint smell of smoke and damp leaves.

He breathes out. "Please, give me a way to find her."

The moon is big and bright but soulless.

Back in the room, Dan lays on the bed, his face on the pillow where Lulu slept. Racing thoughts prevent him from sleeping. He opens his eyes and notices writing on the wall by the pillow. He sits up and switches on the bedside lamp.

Written faintly in pencil he reads:

"And reason mocks my muddled thoughts,
That deaden me to real cares."

And further down:

"My darling pain, both day and night,
You are my intimate delight."

"Lulu," he says.

THE END.

[The poetry in this story is adapted from the poem 'Plead For Me' by Emily Bronte.]

Wuthering Heights

The bell above the door rings and Lulu enters the second-hand bookshop. It smells of dusty paper and old hardbacks. The traffic noise from outside cuts out as the door swings shut. A tall man behind the counter gives a welcoming smile and Lulu smiles back as she walks towards the shelves at the back of the room.

O. O'Brien. O'Connell. She pulls out a book. A painted image of Dan's face fills the cover with the words 'Meeting Bronte by Lulu O'Connell'.

When she released it, she hoped that Dan might discover it and use it to get in touch with her.

"Can I help you?" The man from the reception desk is placing some books on a shelf nearby.

"No, thank you." Lulu places the book back and wanders towards more shelves. B. Bailey, Beckett. Boyd, Bradford, Bronte. Emily Bronte - 'Wuthering Heights'. She takes it and opens the first page. In pencil is the name 'Dan McGregor'. Lulu gasps and drops the book.

"Are you okay?" The shopkeeper looks concerned.

"I'm fine, thank you." She squats down and picks up the book. Again, she opens the first page. It's Dan's handwriting. She looks around. When would he have been here? Is he in town? Does he live nearby? Did the book get passed on by another person?

Lulu leaves through the other pages. Nothing. Just the name in the front.

She puts it back and hurries out the shop.

THE END.

1999

Familiar Eyes

A fierce downpour pounds the pavement
outside Birmingham International Airport and
lashes against the windscreen. The rear lights of
the car in front light up, and a cloud of exhaust
fumes gusts into the night air. Through the
dissipating smoke Dan sees a woman walking
towards him, dressed in a red coat and woollen
hat. She places a case on the pavement next to
his cab.

He steps outside, keeping his face down away from the bitter rain. "Taxi?"

"Yes, please. Western Road," she calls over the noise of the rain. His last fare of the night.

Something about her accent reminds him of someone as he opens the door to let her in.

He starts the engine and tries to put a face to the voice. "Been anywhere nice?"

In his rear-view mirror, he watches as her brow creases in thought, and she removes her hat. "Ireland," she says.

"Lulu."

"Dan?" Lulu gasps and puts her hand over her chest.

It's been eight years.

Her unmistakable Irish lilt transports Dan back to their student days, gigs, drunkenly stumbling around cheap student accommodation, talking and smoking into the early hours.

"How are you?"

"I'm okay."

BEEP! BEEP!

Headlights flash, illuminating the rear window.

"Sorry!" Dan raises his hand and drives forward.

"What are you doing here?" he asks.

"I'm here for a book signing tomorrow."

"A book-signing? Your poetry?"

"It's a novel," she says.

"Wow." Dan shakes his head. "What's it called?"

She hesitates. "Meeting Bronte."

"Sounds interesting. I'll have to get a copy."

Memories flood over Dan like the ephemeral raindrops dashing against the windscreen. The light from passing cars glide over the inside of his taxi.

"I wrote to you," she whispers.

Dan glances in the mirror and sees her beautiful dark familiar eyes. "Yeah, I got your poem, but you didn't put a return address on."

"I put it on the letters."

"The letters?"

"I sent you letters but you didn't reply."

Dan takes a deep breath. "The lease ran out on my house shortly after you left. I didn't get any letters. I did call in every now and then to ask if anything had come but the new tenants weren't interested."

Lulu's eyes widen.

"I tried looking you up," he says, "but I didn't know which village you were from."

They remain silent for a few minutes, the windscreen wipers clearing the raindrops that distort the view. In the rear-view mirror he sees shadows move across her face.

"How have you been?" she asks. "Are you married?"

"No. You?"

"I'm going through a divorce." She looks outside at the passing city landscape.

"Sorry to hear that," he says, as he pulls onto the expressway.

"What have you been doing with yourself? Weren't you thinking of going into the ministry?"

"Yeah, I was a vicar in Haworth for three years."

"Haworth?" She pauses. "I bet you did a wonderful job."

"It's a difficult role. I'm on a break at the moment. It's lasted about two years so far." He waits and then says: "I went to the Wuthering Heights pub on my twenty-fifth birthday."

"I know," she says.

"You know?"

"I went at midnight on the night of your birthday. It was only afterwards that I realised you returned at midnight in the morning. We missed each other. I saw your message on the tree but had no way of finding you."

She opens her purse and asks if she can smoke.

"It's not allowed but feel free."

He sees the end of her cigarette burning in the shadows, and smoke fills the cab. She opens her window a little. "Do you want one?"

"Yeah, thanks."

She hands him the cigarette she's already lit, just like the old days. He takes a deep drag and feels the nicotine rush to his head. He blows the smoke out. "It's been a long time."

"I've been trying to give up," she says.

***

As he pulls up to her house, he tells her he's glad they ran into each other. She opens her purse and pulls out a fifty-pound note for the twenty-pound fare. "Thanks for the lift."

He goes to give her change but she holds up her hand in protest.

"Thanks," he says.

He watches her walk down the path to her house. She pauses and then goes inside without looking back.

Dan holds up the fifty-pound note, and in the corner is a telephone number and a name, Lulu.

THE END

Hello

Light from a streetlamp shines through the transom onto the patterned Minton tile floor of the hallway as Lulu steps down from the staircase. She breathes in the smell of polished wood. The only sound is the steady tick-tock of an antique clock.

She steps through the nearest doorway into a living room. A blue sofa stands against one wall across from a fireplace with a Victorian brass register and marble surround. Shelves of books fill each side: Picasso, Nancy Spero, Art at the Turn of the 21st Century. Cardboard boxes are positioned throughout the room and a photograph leans against one. A picture of Dan taken in his student days. His dark hair is combed back but slightly thinning, sideburns down to the collar of a leather jacket that cover the bottom of his chin. Green eyes with specks of brown look out without giving anything away, like a character from an Edward Hopper painting.

Lulu's phone buzzes and the screen lights up. She doesn't recognize the number.

A message appears: "Hi, it's Dan. I thought I'd get in touch quickly before we lost contact again. Please tell me this is the right number."

Lulu taps a message: "Who is this? Lol. No, it's me Dan. Glad you got in touch. X"

THE END.

2021

Epilogue:

After reading Dan's book, I went back to the Secret Garden with a pen and wrote on the bottom of his story: "I loved your book. I would love to know - is it a true story?"

I left the pen in the plastic wallet so he could reply.

Other people left messages and some reiterated my question. It got posted on social media and received further comments.

I don't know if Dan discovered the responses or not.

On one visit to the smile stones a dog ran through the woods behind me. I heard a whistle and through the trees glimpsed a bearded man in a green bomber jacket, black jeans and hiking boots. He whistled again and the dog followed. I'm convinced it was him, but I guess I'll never know, unless one day I manage to speak to him or Lulu.

Soundtrack:

Folsom Prison Blues
By Johnny Cash

Raspberry Beret
By Prince & The Revolution

The Killing Moon
By Echo & The Bunnymen

Walk This Way
By Run DMC

Gypsy Woman
By Crystal Waters

Glory Box
By Portishead

Lovesong
By The Cure

Unforgettable
By Nat King Cole

No Ordinary Love
By Sade

The Secret Garden
By Bruce Springsteen

Also available:

'Short Stories of Love & Entanglement' by Andy Houstoun

'How to write Short Stories of Love & Entanglement' by Andy Houstoun

Printed in Great Britain
by Amazon